THE
MAGNIFICENT
⇥ BOOK ⇤
OF
DRAGONS

THE
MAGNIFICENT
❖ BOOK ❖
OF
DRAGONS

ILLUSTRATED BY
Gonzalso Kenny

WRITTEN BY
Stella Caldwell

Written by Stella Caldwell
Illustrated by Gonzalo Kenny

Published by Weldon Owen Children's Books
An imprint of Weldon Owen International, L.P.
A subsidiary of Insight International, L.P.
PO Box 3088
San Rafael, CA 94912
www.insighteditions.com

Weldon Owen Children's Books:
Edited by Diana Craig
Assistant Editor: Pandita Geary
Senior Production Manager: Greg Steffen
Art Director: Stuart Smith
Publisher: Sue Grabham

Insight Editions:
Publisher: Raoul Goff

ISBN: 978-1-68188-769-2
Manufactured, printed, and assembled in China
First printing, October 2021. STR/10/21
23 22 21 20 19 1 2 3 4 5
ISBN: 978-1-68188-739-5

INTRODUCTION

What do you think of when you hear the word "dragon"? Perhaps you picture a fire-breathing monster with fearsome claws and beating wings? Or do you imagine a long, serpentlike creature with enormous eyes like the dragons in Chinese New Year celebrations? These incredible creatures come in many other shapes and sizes too. Find out which have been conquered and slayed, and which are still found in the world's rivers, seas, mountains, and skies.

The Magnificent Book of Dragons takes you on a quest to the four corners of the world to meet flying monsters, water serpents, and creatures that lurk in dark lairs. Marvel at hundred-headed Typhon, or the mighty Tiamat, dragon-goddess of the ocean. Discover the deadly basilisk, who can kill with a single glance. Learn how eating the magical heart of the dragon Fafnir could give you great wisdom.

Meet Zmey Gorynich, the terrifying mountain dragon with three fire-spitting heads. Voyage to the depths of the ocean to discover a dragon in a palace made of coral and jewels. Encounter a monster who can swallow the sun, dragons who create rainbows, a serpent who rains gold, and a feathered snake who can disguise himself as the Morning Star.

AT A GLANCE

WHERE IN THE WORLD? India

APPEARANCE: Huge body and jaws

LAIR: Mountaintops

BEHAVIOR: Wicked and loathsome

DRAGON POWER: Ninety-nine superstrong coils

Embark on a magical journey to meet some of the most magnificent dragons in the world.

CONTENTS

TIAMAT

Tiamat was an enormous dragon that lived long before the world was made. There was no land or sky, just a vast ocean. The ancient Babylonians believed that Tiamat was the goddess of this ocean.

This mighty sea serpent had a long, thrashing tail and huge horns. Her skin was so thick and tough that nothing could pierce it.

🐉 Tiamat's husband was Apzu, the god of fresh water. Together, they created new gods, but these gods killed Apzu. In her fury, Tiamat made eleven monsters, including the Viper, the Great Lion, and the Storm Demon.

🐉 The first dragons were Tiamat's children. These snarling beasts had poison running through their veins instead of blood.

🐉 The god Marduk fought a great battle with Tiamat. His weapons were the four winds and a bow that could shoot bolts of lightning. He killed Tiamat by hurling a howling storm into her gaping jaws.

🐉 After her death, Tiamat's body was sliced in two to become the sky and the earth. Her tail became the Milky Way, and the world's great rivers were made from her eyes.

AT A GLANCE

WHERE IN THE WORLD? Babylonia (modern Iraq)

APPEARANCE: Gigantic serpent

LAIR: Deep in the salty sea

BEHAVIOR: Jealous and destructive

DRAGON POWER: Gave birth to terrifying monsters

TYPHON

 Gigantic Typhon is perhaps the most monstrous dragon of all. An army of writhing serpents rises from his shoulders, each of them belching fire and spitting poison.

 The monster's one hundred heads have black, flickering tongues and flashing eyes. Their dreadful hissing is so loud, it can be heard across mountains.

 Typhon's mother is the Greek goddess Gaia. His father is Tartarus, the god of a black pit deep underground. The ancient Greeks believed this was where wicked people went when they died.

 Typhon's wife is a cave-dwelling dragoness called Echidna. She is half-woman and half-serpent.

 This enormous Greek dragon has many terrifying children. They include the three-headed dog called Cerberus, the goat-headed Chimera, and the fearsome Colchian Dragon.

AT A GLANCE

WHERE IN THE WORLD? Sicily, Italy

APPEARANCE: Hundred-headed

LAIR: Deep beneath Mount Etna

BEHAVIOR: Flies into stormy rages

DRAGON POWER: Causes volcanic eruptions and creates typhoons

Long ago, the Greek god Zeus battled Typhon and crushed him beneath Mount Etna, a volcano in Sicily. Typhon is still there. When he rages, he spews fire and lava from the volcano's mouth.

 Typhon is sometimes described as a storm giant. He can whip up dangerous winds called typhoons and send them out into the world.

SHENLONG

This majestic Chinese dragon rules the wind and the rain. He may bring gentle showers or soothing breezes. But when he is angry, Shenlong whips up terrifying storms and sends great floods.

This dragon's enormous body stretches right across the sky. He doesn't have wings, but uses his magical powers to fly through the clouds.

Magnificent staglike antlers rise up from Shenlong's proud head, and glittering blue scales cover his long body. They shimmer and sparkle, and could blind your eyes when the sun is shining brightly.

Shenlong has four short legs, with five rather than four claws on each foot. Only really important Chinese dragons have five claws on their feet.

Shenlong hatched from an egg that was three thousand years old. The egg couldn't hatch until it had spent a thousand years in the water, a thousand years in the mountains, and a thousand years in the sun.

This shape-shifting dragon can change his form. If Shenlong feels tired, he transforms himself into a tiny mouse and hides away. This infuriates the god of thunder, who sends flashes of lightning to find him.

AT A GLANCE

WHERE IN THE WORLD? China

APPEARANCE: Shimmering blue scales, staglike antlers

LAIR: Above the clouds

BEHAVIOR: Moody and changeable

DRAGON POWER: Controls the weather

THE COLCHIAN DRAGON

- The menacing Colchian Dragon never sleeps, even for a second! His flamelike eyes are always watching. Nothing escapes his terrible gaze.

- Three flickering tongues dart in and out of the monster's great jaws. He has an enormous crest on top of his head, which makes him look even more terrifying.

- The Colchian Dragon blasts out searing-hot plumes of fire—just like his father, the monster Typhon.

- Tough, horny scales cover this creature's gigantic body. As he slithers along the ground, his tail makes a strange rattling noise.

- The dragon gets his name from Colchis, the ancient Greek region where he was born.

- In ancient times, the dragon guarded a magical ram's coat called the Golden Fleece. The Greek hero Jason was sent to steal this treasure. He succeeded by putting the dragon to sleep with an enchanted potion.

- This monster has a set of magical teeth. If you plant them in the soil, a fierce band of warriors will spring up from the ground.

AT A GLANCE

WHERE IN THE WORLD? Greece

APPEARANCE: Serpentine, three-tongued

LAIR: An oak tree

BEHAVIOR: Never sleeps

DRAGON POWER: Has magical teeth

THE LERNAEAN HYDRA

- The enormous, snakelike Hydra lived thousands of years ago in the region of Lerna in ancient Greece. She had nine horrifying heads. If anyone tried to cut one off, two more sprouted in its place!

- This water serpent made her lair in a foul-smelling swamp. Here, she guarded a cave that led down to Hades, which was the Greek underground world of the dead.

- At night, the Hydra crept from her lair and greedily feasted on cattle and passing humans. Those who escaped being eaten alive were killed by the dragon's deadly breath.

- The Greek hero Heracles killed the Hydra with the help of his nephew Iolaus. Heracles sliced off the dragon's heads, and Iolaus burned the stumps to stop them from regrowing.

When the Hydra died, the Greek goddess Hera placed her body in the heavens and changed her into a constellation called the Hydra. At night you can still see the dragon winding her starry tail across the sky.

AT A GLANCE

WHERE IN THE WORLD? Greece

APPEARANCE: Nine-headed

LAIR: Swamp next to Hades

BEHAVIOR: Savage and selfish

DRAGON POWER: Grew new heads

THE GREAT FIREDRAKE

- The Great Firedrake lived long ago in Scandinavia. His lair was a deep, dark cave, where he guarded a mound of glittering treasure. The fabulous hoard included gold and silver coins, and weapons set with jewels.

- A thief once stole a golden goblet from the Firedrake. The beast flew into a terrible rage. Bellowing with anger, he traveled the length of the land, destroying everything in sight.

- The Firedrake had a lizardlike body, four short legs, and huge wings. He could dart rapidly across the ground and fly great distances.

- The dragon's most fearsome weapon was the fire that billowed from his mighty jaws.

AT A GLANCE

WHERE IN THE WORLD?
Scandinavia

APPEARANCE: Lizardlike, winged

LAIR: A dark cave

BEHAVIOR: Only active at night

DRAGON POWER: Spewed flames

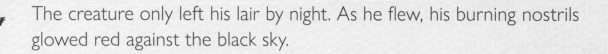 The creature only left his lair by night. As he flew, his burning nostrils glowed red against the black sky.

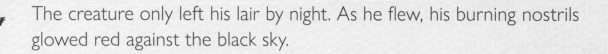 Enormous, curved fangs glistened in the dragon's jaws. His venom was deadly, and no creature could survive his bite.

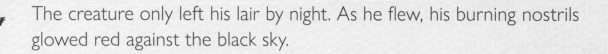 The Norse hero Beowulf battled the Firedrake. Beowulf's armor protected him from the dragon's fiery breath, but the beast sank his teeth into the warrior's neck. Both Beowulf and the dragon died of their wounds.

THE JACULUS

- The European jaculus sits silently in the trees and watches for any passing animal or human. It swiftly leaps out at its unfortunate victim and delivers a brutal blow to the back of its head.

- Leafy trees or bushes are where a jaculus makes its lair. The creature's green scales blend in with the leaves, giving excellent camouflage. Sometimes, though, its glowing eyes reveal where it is hiding.

- The dragon's two short legs look stumpy, but they are incredibly strong. They help the creature to leap from tree to tree, and to hurl itself at prey.

- If danger threatens, a jaculus can coil itself into a tight ball. Its tough scales are like a coat of armor.

- This dragon is sometimes known as the javelin snake because it can sail through the air like a javelin spear. A jaculus hits its target with such force that it can knock itself out, or even fall dead to the ground.

- The jaws of a jaculus are small, but they are lined with serrated teeth. If the dragon's strike fails to kill a victim, its ferocious bite finishes the job.

- During the breeding season, a male jaculus flies short distances to hunt for a mate. The female lays her eggs in a large nest of twigs and rears one or two young.

AT A GLANCE

WHERE IN THE WORLD? Europe

APPEARANCE: Small and powerful

LAIR: Leafy trees and bushes

BEHAVIOR: Stealthy and secretive

DRAGON POWER: Kills with a single strike

THE DRAGON OF SILENE

This North African dragon lived hundreds of years ago near the city of Silene in Libya. He had a ferocious appetite. This hungry beast ate all the sheep in the area, and then he began to feast on people.

The monster made his lair at the bottom of a very deep lake. Whenever he moved, he stirred up enormous waves that crashed across the water.

AT A GLANCE

WHERE IN THE WORLD? Libya, Africa

APPEARANCE: Winged, two-legged

LAIR: A deep lake

BEHAVIOR: Hungry for human flesh

DRAGON POWER: Blasted poison and flames

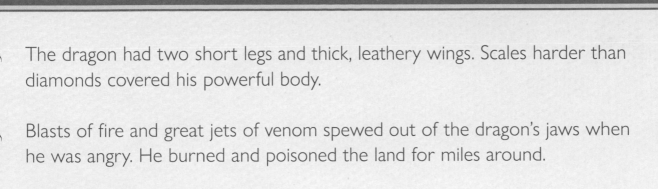

The dragon had two short legs and thick, leathery wings. Scales harder than diamonds covered his powerful body.

Blasts of fire and great jets of venom spewed out of the dragon's jaws when he was angry. He burned and poisoned the land for miles around.

The dragon's daggerlike talons were so sharp, they could cut through a knight's armor.

A brave knight called St. George was determined to slay the dragon, but his spear couldn't pierce the monster's scales. He finally succeeded by thrusting his weapon into a tiny patch of skin under the beast's wing.

BIDA

- This gigantic black serpent from West Africa made his lair in a deep, dark cave. When hungry, he simply stuck his head out of his cave and grasped a passing human in his savage jaws.

- Bida had the ability to fly at great speed. A dreadful shadow passed over the land when his huge, snaking body flew past the sun.

- The people living nearby made an agreement with Bida. They brought human victims directly to the serpent's cave. In return, Bida flew through the skies and made it rain gold three times a year.

- Bida's frightful hiss was so terrifying that animals for miles around scattered at the sound of it. When angered, the serpent spat out huge clouds of deadly venom that killed any living thing it touched.

The serpent was greedy not only for human flesh, but also for treasure. Piles of gold coins shimmered beneath his glossy coils, while human bones lay scattered around his lair.

Before snatching a victim, Bida always stuck his head out of his cave three times. Long ago, a brave man waited outside the cave and sliced off the beast's head the third time it appeared. The dying Bida cursed the land with a terrible drought.

AT A GLANCE

WHERE IN THE WORLD? West Africa

APPEARANCE: Black, snakelike

LAIR: A deep cave

BEHAVIOR: Malicious and unforgiving

DRAGON POWER: Rained down gold

FUTS-LONG

- This magnificent Chinese dragon makes his lair deep underground. He sometimes rises to the Earth's surface, causing volcanoes to erupt and spew out flames and lava.

- Deep orange scales cover the dragon's snakelike body. His eyes blaze with fire, and the four claws on each of his feet shine like silver.

- Futs-Long is a treasure dragon. He guards the Earth's riches, keeping watch over valuable gems and metals.

- Like many Chinese dragons, Futs-Long is a peaceful creature unless he is offended. Earthquakes are a sign that he is angry. His furious roars make the ground shake and cause great cracks to appear on its surface.

- The teeth of this dragon contain powerful magic. They can be ground into a fine powder and used in spells and potions.

- Beneath the creature's chin is a precious pearl of wisdom. The gem contains fragments of the sun, moon, and stars, and gleams in the darkness. Only the very wisest dragons have such a pearl.

- Futs-Long has many magical powers. He can become invisible, or shape-shift into any form he wishes. Sometimes he shrinks to the size of a flea, or he might grow as big as the sky.

AT A GLANCE

WHERE IN THE WORLD? China

APPEARANCE: Snakelike, fiery scales

LAIR: Deep underground

BEHAVIOR: Wise and trustworthy

DRAGON POWER: Can change shape or become invisible

THE BASILISK

- A basilisk can kill with a single glance. Any creature foolish enough to meet its eyes will drop dead on the spot.

- This dragon has a white, crownlike marking on its head. It doesn't slither along the ground like other serpents, but holds the front part of its body upright at all times.

- Basilisks are not especially large or powerful-looking, but their deafening hiss is truly terrifying. Even other serpents scatter at the sound.

- These creatures are found in Europe. They prefer desertlike regions and make their lairs in shallow holes. Their scorching breath sets shrubs and grass on fire.

- The air around a basilisk is so poisonous that birds flying overhead plunge from the sky, stone-dead.

- Baby basilisks hatch from the eggs of toads, but only if those eggs have been brooded, or kept warm, by a cockerel.

There are only two creatures in the world that a basilisk cannot harm. The weasel cannot be killed by the monster's deadly stare and venom. A crowing cock will make a basilisk collapse and shrivel up.

AT A GLANCE

WHERE IN THE WORLD? Europe

APPEARANCE: Cobralike serpent

LAIR: A desert hole

BEHAVIOR: Proud and kinglike

DRAGON POWER: Fatal gaze

THE RED DRAGON

- The magnificent Red Dragon of Wales is one of the fiercest creatures in the world. He has a long memory and never forgives an enemy.

- Shimmering scales cover the dragon's enormous body. They are hot to touch and glow red in the dark. If a scale falls away from the creature's body, it can burst into flames and start a fire.

- The thunderous beating of this dragon's huge wings can be heard for many miles around. The monster uses the hooked claws on his wing tips to fight other dragons in the air.

- If angered, the Red Dragon blasts out plumes of blistering fire. He is a very proud creature, and may belch out flames just to prove his might.

AT A GLANCE

WHERE IN THE WORLD? Wales

APPEARANCE: Winged, four-legged

LAIR: Mountains and caves

BEHAVIOR: Proud and courageous

DRAGON POWER: Scales that start fires

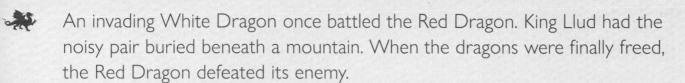

An invading White Dragon once battled the Red Dragon. King Llud had the noisy pair buried beneath a mountain. When the dragons were finally freed, the Red Dragon defeated its enemy.

The Red Dragon has been used as a symbol of Wales for more than 1,300 years. He represents the proud, fierce spirit of the Welsh people.

THE TATZELWURM

The nightmarish tatzelwurm, or claw worm, prowls the Alpine mountains of Europe. It is hardly ever seen, although walkers sometimes hear its bloodcurdling howls.

A tatzelwurm has a face like a ferocious cat and a body like a lizard. Its two stumpy legs have razor-clawed feet. The creature usually feasts on livestock, although it will also attack humans.

By day, tatzelwurms hide out in remote wooded areas or stalk snowy mountain peaks. If cornered, they will hiss savagely and launch a vicious attack.

When a tatzelwurm attacks, it makes a high-pitched whistling noise. The dreadful sound is like sharp fingernails scratching a metal surface.

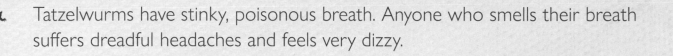 Tatzelwurms have stinky, poisonous breath. Anyone who smells their breath suffers dreadful headaches and feels very dizzy.

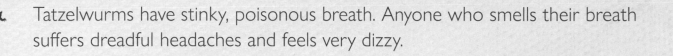 Some people have described how a tatzelwurm can rear itself up to become taller than a human. The creature can also leap several yards in the air.

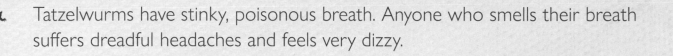 A Swiss village was once terrorized by a tatzelwurm. Each night, it savaged sheep and sucked all the milk from the villagers' cows. Eventually, the people laid a trap and managed to kill the beast.

AT A GLANCE

WHERE IN THE WORLD? European Alps

APPEARANCE: Cat-headed, lizardlike

LAIR: Mountain caves and hollows

BEHAVIOR: Shy but ferocious

DRAGON POWER: Can suck livestock dry

APALALA

- Apalala is a good-natured dragon in spite of his fierce looks. He has a huge serpent's body and tail and the head of a man. His grinning mouth is lined with pointed teeth.

- The creature is found in Pakistan, in a valley around the Swat River. The river obeys Apalala's every command, as do the wind and the rain.

- Although Apalala doesn't have wings, he has magical flying powers. As he soars through the skies, his powerful eyes can see everything on the ground below.

- A long fin runs down Apalala's back. This helps him to dart quickly through the river like a fish.

- The dragon's sharp, hooked talons are powerful weapons. He uses them to fight other dragons. They can tear and rip through anything.

- Apalala brings gentle rain to help the crops grow. But if people are ungrateful, he sends terrible floods that cause great damage. Sometimes, he stops the rain altogether so that crops wither and dry.

- This dragon belongs to a group of Asian dragons called nagas. These water creatures are usually half-serpent and half-human. They can be helpful to people, as well as dangerous and powerful.

AT A GLANCE

WHERE IN THE WORLD? Pakistan

APPEARANCE: Human head, serpent's body

LAIR: The Swat River

BEHAVIOR: Kindhearted and helpful

DRAGON POWER: Controls the river, wind, and rain

QUETZALCOATL

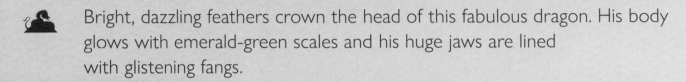

- Bright, dazzling feathers crown the head of this fabulous dragon. His body glows with emerald-green scales and his huge jaws are lined with glistening fangs.

- The name Quetzalcoatl means "plumed serpent". The Aztec people, who once lived in central Mexico, worshipped Quetzalcoatl as a wise and important creator god.

- The Aztecs believed that Quetzalcoatl and his brother Tezcatlipoca created the Earth from the body of a serpent called Cipactli. They made trees and flowers from her hair and skin, and caves and springs from her eyes and nose.

- Quetzelcoatl can turn himself into the Morning Star. You can see him in the sky before the sun rises. His twin brother, Xolotl, is the evening star.

- Quetzalcoatl once traveled to the underworld to collect the ancient bones of the dead. He poured blood on them to create new people to fill our world.

AT A GLANCE

WHERE IN THE WORLD? Mexico

APPEARANCE: Dazzling feathers and emerald-green scales

LAIR: The sky

BEHAVIOR: Wise and fierce

DRAGON POWER: Can turn into the Morning Star

This serpent god can control the wind and rain. The Aztecs believed that when the sky darkens and the wind blows in many directions, it is a sign of Quetzalcoatl's fury.

 The Aztecs built the Great Pyramid of Cholula in Mexico for Quetzalcoatl. It is the largest pyramid in the world, four times bigger than the Great Pyramid of Egypt.

FAFNIR

- The Norse dragon Fafnir lived long ago. He was born a dwarf and was the son of Hreidmar, the king of the dwarves.

- Fafnir the dwarf stole his father's gold and went off to hide in a cold mountain cave. There, he guarded his glittering pile of treasure, and gradually changed from a dwarf into an enormous, spiteful dragon.

- The monster had a long, scaly body and two short legs. His huge tail coiled right around his cave. He greedily devoured any person who dared to come near.

- Each day, Fafnir lumbered from his lair to drink from a nearby stream. The gigantic tracks he left on the muddy bank terrified anyone who saw them.

AT A GLANCE

WHERE IN THE WORLD? Scandinavia

APPEARANCE: Huge, two-legged

LAIR: A dark, damp cave

BEHAVIOR: Greedy and vile

DRAGON POWER: Magical heart

Glittering, bladelike fangs jutted from Fafnir's jaws and his yellow eyes burned with greed. His fiery breath poisoned everything around him.

Fafnir's heart had magical powers. It was said that anyone who ate it would have great wisdom, and even understand the speech of birds.

Long ago, the Norse hero Sigurd set out to slay Fafnir. He lay in a pit near the dragon's cave and waited. When Fafnir passed over Sigurd's hiding place, the hero drove his sword deep into the beast's soft belly.

ZMEY GORYNICH

- This dragon was one of the most horrifying monsters that ever lived. He had three fire-spitting heads, and his body was so enormous that it could block out the sun.

- Having three heads meant that the creature could do several things at once. While one head kept watch, another belched fire and the third let out terrifying roars.

- The name Zmey Gorynich means "snake of the mountains". He lived hundreds of years ago, high up on snowy mountain peaks. When hungry, the monster came down to the villages to hunt for human flesh.

- Powerful back legs allowed the monster to walk upright, leaving his shorter forelimbs free. These ended in curved copper claws that could rip through anything.

The monster had seven tails with sharp spikes at their tips. He used these deadly weapons like whips to lash at prey. One strike was enough to send a creature hurtling through the air.

Leathery wings enabled the dragon to glide through the air, rather than fly long distances.

A Russian warrior battled for three days with Zmey Gorynich. He slayed the beast but then found he was swimming in the dragon's blood. After three days, the blood seeped away and the warrior survived.

AT A GLANCE

WHERE IN THE WORLD? Russia

APPEARANCE: Three-headed, winged

LAIR: Snowy mountaintops

BEHAVIOR: Loud and boastful

DRAGON POWER: Seven lashing tails

JÖRMUNGANDR

- This fearsome serpent lives in the ocean. He is said to be so enormous that he can wrap himself around the whole world and grasp his own tail in his mouth.

- Jörmungandr is the child of the Norse giantess Angrboda and a mischievous god called Loki. His brother is a huge, savage wolf called Fenrir. His sister is Hel, the goddess of the dead.

- When Jörmungandr rages, the ocean becomes wild and stormy. He flashes fire from his eyes and sprays huge jets of poison up into the sky.

- Viking sailors were terrified of Jörmungandr as they traveled across the seas more than a thousand years ago. They believed that the serpent could rise up from the depths and crush their ships in his huge jaws.

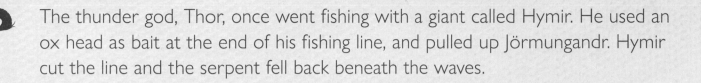

The thunder god, Thor, once went fishing with a giant called Hymir. He used an ox head as bait at the end of his fishing line, and pulled up Jörmungandr. Hymir cut the line and the serpent fell back beneath the waves.

The Vikings believed that one day Jörmungandr will thrash his way out of the ocean and Ragnarok will begin. This will be the end of the world, when giants attack the gods, and wolves swallow the sun and the moon.

AT A GLANCE

WHERE IN THE WORLD? Scandinavia

APPEARANCE: Long enough to circle the world

LAIR: Deep in the ocean

BEHAVIOR: Powerful and terrifying

DRAGON POWER: Creates raging storms and crushes ships

THE WAWEL DRAGON

This hungry dragon lived hundreds of years ago in a deep cave on Wawel Hill, near Kraków in Poland. No matter how many people he gulped down, there was always room for another.

Apart from humans, the dragon's favorite food was sheep or pigs. His jaws were so huge, he could devour an animal in one greedy mouthful. The monster drooled as he feasted on his prey.

When the beast wasn't eating, he was spitting out great plumes of fire. The countryside for miles around was blackened and burned.

The Wawel Dragon roared and bellowed when he was angry, rearing up on his enormous hind legs. He used his shorter front limbs to claw and grasp at prey.

The creature's powerful eyes burned like hot coals. His incredible vision allowed him to see for many miles. He could spot the tiniest movement, even in the blackness of his cave.

Many people tried to kill the monster, but in vain. Their arrows and swords shattered against the creature's iron-hard scales.

AT A GLANCE

WHERE IN THE WORLD? Poland

APPEARANCE: Four-legged, winged

LAIR: Deep, dark cave

BEHAVIOR: Hot-tempered and violent

DRAGON POWER: Could see for miles

A clever shoemaker finally thought of a way to kill the dragon by leaving him a poisoned lamb to eat. As soon as the beast ate it, he felt a burning fire in his belly. To cool the fire, he drank so much river water that he burst.

APEP

This dreadful serpent was the ancient Egyptian god of chaos and darkness. When he roared, terrifying storms battered the land and earthquakes violently shook the ground.

Apep lived in the ancient Egyptian underworld of the dead, called Duat. The Egyptian people called him Eater of Souls. They used spells when they buried their dead to protect them from the monster's evil power.

The serpent was the great enemy of the sun god, Ra. Each day, Ra passed through the sky in his boat before entering the underworld at nightfall. Every night, Apep tried to kill Ra and prevent sunrise, but without success.

This evil beast measured many miles in length. His head was made of flint, which is a type of very hard stone.

The ancient Egyptians made wax models of Apep and burned them, or drew pictures of him and spat on them. They hoped these rituals would keep the monster away.

The serpent was sometimes called the Evil Lizard or the Destroyer.

Occasionally, Apep swallowed the sun god, Ra. This plunged the world into darkness, an event known as a solar eclipse. Fortunately, the other gods always cut Ra free and the sun shone again.

AT A GLANCE

WHERE IN THE WORLD? Egypt

APPEARANCE: Miles long, head of stone

LAIR: The ancient Egyptian underworld

BEHAVIOR: Dark and evil

DRAGON POWER: Could swallow the sun

THE LOCH NESS MONSTER

- This monster lurks in the cold depths of Loch Ness, a huge lake in the north of Scotland. She is also known as Nessie.

- The deep and murky waters of Loch Ness are the perfect place for this mysterious beast to hide. She is hardly ever seen, but sometimes her head breaks through the loch's calm surface.

- Nessie has a very long neck, a snakelike body, and four paddlelike limbs. She uses her front limbs to move swiftly through the water, while her back limbs help with steering.

The creature's head is quite small compared to her huge body. Her long, narrow jaws are crammed with dagger-sharp teeth.

The loch froths and bubbles when the Loch Ness monster rises up from the depths. Waves crash across the surface, and boats are tossed into the air.

A monk called St. Columba was the first person known to have seen the creature, around 1,500 years ago. He described how he saw a monster about to attack a swimmer. He commanded it to "go back", and it did.

The monster sometimes creeps out of the loch onto dry land. People say they have seen her dragging herself across the road or crashing through the bushes. Sometimes, giant tracks are found along the shore.

AT A GLANCE

WHERE IN THE WORLD: Scotland

APPEARANCE: Long neck, serpent body

LAIR: The depths of Loch Ness

BEHAVIOR: Secretive and mysterious

DRAGON POWER: Stays hidden

THE COCKATRICE

- This fabulous dragon-bird has a cockerel's head, a serpent's body, and batlike wings. Just one glance from its eyes can turn you to stone.

- The cockatrice has many weapons. Its fiery breath can scorch a victim, while its clawed "hands" scratch and tear. The cockatrice's stinking, poisonous breath can kill any living thing.

- Cockatrices do not lay their own eggs. A baby cockatrice hatches from a cockerel's egg, but only if that egg has been brooded, or kept warm, by a toad or a snake.

- There is only one way to prevent the birth of a cockatrice. If you find an egg, toss it right over your house without breaking it!

- The cockatrice keeps well away from the weasel, which is its deadly enemy. This creature can easily defeat a cockatrice.

- An old story from 1794 tells how a vicious cockatrice flew out of the church ruins in Renwick, an English village. The villagers killed it with a rowan branch, which is said to keep witches away.

- To kill a cockatrice, hold a mirror up to it. If the dragon catches sight of its own eyes, it will fall down dead.

AT A GLANCE

WHERE IN THE WORLD? Europe

APPEARANCE: Half-serpent, half-bird

LAIR: Dark, damp areas

BEHAVIOR: Always stirring up trouble

DRAGON POWER: Turns victims to stone

NIDHOGG

- The dragon Nidhogg lives underground, chewing at the roots of a huge, magical ash tree called Yggdrasil. In Viking times, it was believed that the roots and branches of Yggdrasil held the whole world together.

- The name Nidhogg means "dread biter." The dragon has enormous, glistening teeth, and never stops gnashing and gnawing.

- Tough, gnarled scales cover the creature's enormous body. His eyes burn like lamps in the darkness of his underground lair.

- The dragon only leaves his lair to visit Niflheim, the foggy underworld home of the dead. In this cold, shadowy place, he greedily feasts on the bodies of dead people.

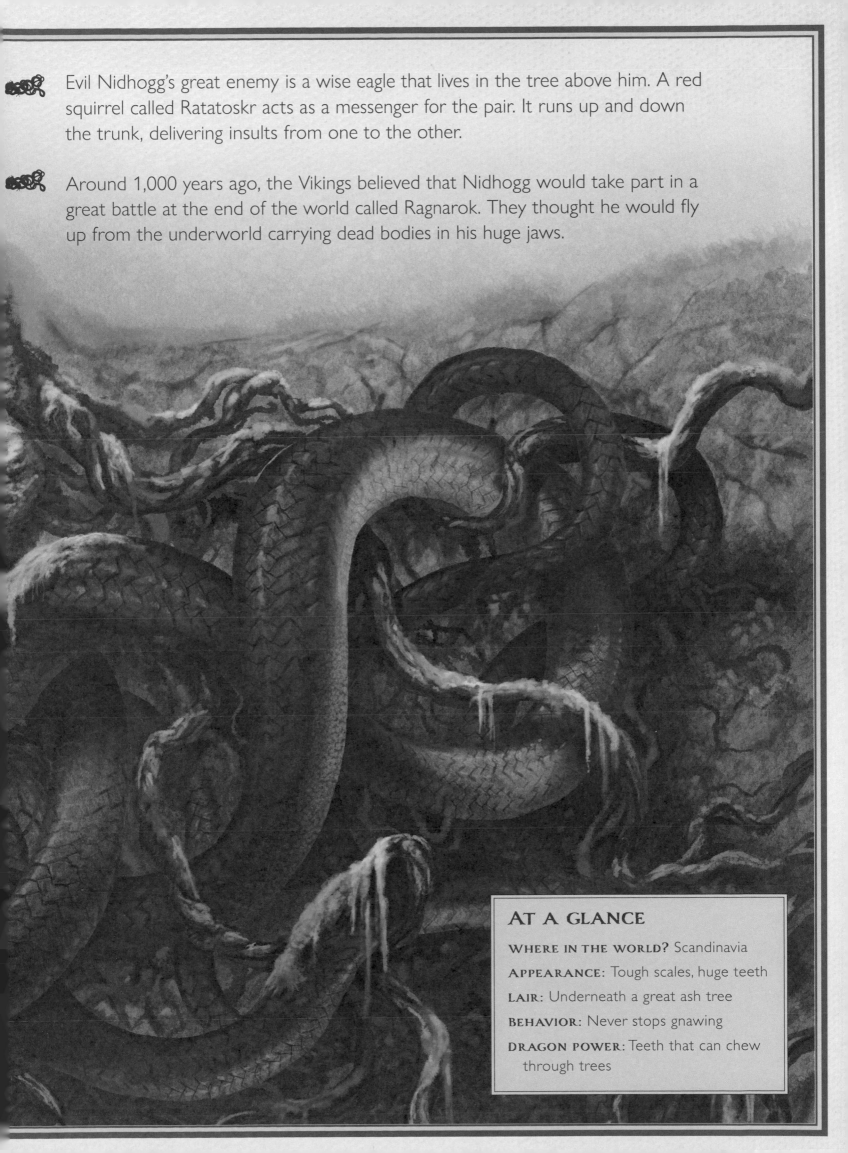

Evil Nidhogg's great enemy is a wise eagle that lives in the tree above him. A red squirrel called Ratatoskr acts as a messenger for the pair. It runs up and down the trunk, delivering insults from one to the other.

Around 1,000 years ago, the Vikings believed that Nidhogg would take part in a great battle at the end of the world called Ragnarok. They thought he would fly up from the underworld carrying dead bodies in his huge jaws.

AT A GLANCE

WHERE IN THE WORLD? Scandinavia

APPEARANCE: Tough scales, huge teeth

LAIR: Underneath a great ash tree

BEHAVIOR: Never stops gnawing

DRAGON POWER: Teeth that can chew through trees

YAMATA NO OROCHI

Eight hissing heads and eight writhing tails gave this Japanese dragon his name, which means "eight-forked serpent". His body was so huge that it coiled around eight hills and stretched across eight valleys.

This serpent had a terrible thirst for human blood. He was constantly hungry, and his huge belly bulged with the weight of his unlucky victims.

It was easy to walk right past Yamata no Orochi without realizing he was there. Fir and cypress trees sprouted from his broad back, and thick moss coated his scales. He looked just like a harmless, tree-covered mountain.

AT A GLANCE

WHERE IN THE WORLD? Japan

APPEARANCE: Eight heads and tails

LAIR: Hilltops and valleys

BEHAVIOR: Greedy and grasping

DRAGON POWER: Master of disguise

The serpent's sixteen red eyes were as red as cherries. They could see in every direction, and were constantly looking out for their next meal.

Susanoo, the god of storms, finally killed the dragon by tempting him with eight huge barrels of a wine called saké. Yamata no Orochi drank the liquid and fell into a deep, drunken sleep. Susanoo chopped off his eight heads.

A magical sword called the Heavenly Sword of Gathering Clouds was found buried in one of the serpent's tails. Any warrior that holds this precious weapon will be given great bravery and be protected from harm.

THE KNUCKER

This sly dragon hides in deep, murky ponds called knuckerholes. Beware of falling into one, as knuckerholes are bottomless.

It can be hard to spot a knucker. Like a crocodile, it lets only its eyes and snout show above the water as it waits for its next meal. When prey passes by, the dragon lunges at it with lightning speed.

A long, serpentlike body allows the knucker to slide through water like an eel. Its short wings are not used for flying, but they help the creature to swim.

Sharp little teeth line the dragon's snapping jaws. The knucker's venom is extremely poisonous and causes an intense, burning pain to its victims.

The female lays her eggs in damp leaves near her knuckerhole. After hatching, the baby dragons rapidly make their way to the safety of water. They slither along the ground like little snakes.

The knucker makes an unpleasant hissing noise when it is threatened. If it is particularly angry or hungry, its furious bellowing can be heard for miles around.

Long ago, a famous knucker lived in the English village of Lyminster. It hid in its deep knuckerhole, snatching and devouring people. Eventually, a boy called Jim Pulk killed the greedy beast by giving it a poisoned pie.

AT A GLANCE

WHERE IN THE WORLD? England

APPEARANCE: Snakelike, short wings

LAIR: A watery "knuckerhole"

BEHAVIOR: Sly and shifty

DRAGON POWER: Creates bottomless ponds to catch victims

RYŪJIN

This Japanese dragon is master of the ocean. He is a fair ruler who brings pleasant winds and gentle rains. But just one angry thrash of his mighty tail creates wild and stormy seas.

Ryūjin's body is covered in deep blue scales. Magnificent horns rise from his head, while his long whiskers are a sign of great wisdom. It is said that his dazzling appearance is fatal to human eyes.

Powerful whirlpools form when Ryūjin opens his enormous mouth. Whales and even great ships are sucked down into his gaping jaws.

AT A GLANCE

WHERE IN THE WORLD? Japan

APPEARANCE: Blue scales, horned

LAIR: Glittering ocean palace

BEHAVIOR: Noble and just

DRAGON POWER: Controls the tides

Ryūjin has a palace under the sea, which is made of beautiful corals and glitters with jewels. Legend has it that just a single day in this palace is as long as a hundred years on Earth.

Giant turtles, colorful fish, and even jellyfish are the dragon's loyal servants. They wait on their king, carrying out his every command.

This ruler of the seas owns two fabulous, magical jewels. With one jewel, he can make the tide go out. With the other, he draws the tide back in. The jewels can cause great floods and huge tidal waves.

Around three hundred years ago, the Japanese warrior Tawara Toda saved Ryūjin's palace from a flesh-eating centipede. The horrifying creature was as long as a mountain. Ryūjin gave the hero a bronze bell as a reward.

WYVERN

- The ferocious wyvern has a powerful, scaly body, leathery, batlike wings, and strange, mesmerizing eyes. Its hypnotic stare can lure helpless prey straight into its waiting jaws!

- Although it can't breathe fire, the wyvern is a fierce hunter. It has eaglelike talons, razor-sharp teeth, and a diamond-shaped barb, or hook, on the tip of its tail.

- Unlike many other winged dragons, the wyvern has two legs rather than four.

- The wyvern's name can be traced back to the Latin word *vipera*, which means "viper." Vipers are snakes with long, poisonous fangs.

- The Mordiford Wyvern was an English dragon that lived more than five hundred years ago. A girl called Maud found him as a baby and looked after him. As he grew bigger, he began killing livestock and people. He was finally slain by a nobleman called Garston.

A wyvern called Thyrus once terrorized the people of Terni in Italy. He attacked anyone who crossed his path, and poisoned the air with his stinking breath. In the end, a young man from Terni killed him.

The wyvern is a common symbol on old coats of arms from hundreds of years ago. It represented courage, strength, and, sometimes, revenge.

AT A GLANCE

WHERE IN THE WORLD? Europe

APPEARANCE: Winged, two-legged

LAIR. Forests and marshes

BEHAVIOR: Cunning and merciless

DRAGON POWER: Hypnotic eyes

BOITATÁ

- Crackling flames cover the body of this giant serpent. At night, the creature creates an incredible blazing trail as he slithers through the darkness.

- Boitatá lives in the dense jungles of Brazil. He hides during the day, as his eyesight is very poor in sunlight. At night, he creeps from his lair and crawls across open fields in search of prey.

- The serpent's enormous eyes burn like lanterns in the darkness. Lost travelers sometimes follow these lights, hoping to find safety. Instead, they are led straight to the hungry Boitatá!

The creature's tracks are easy to spot. The grass will be scorched where he has passed by, and even nearby trees may be blackened.

The serpent attacks livestock and humans. Sometimes he uses his large, bulllike horns to gore a victim. He can also coil his gigantic body around prey and slowly squeeze it to death.

Although the serpent's bite is not poisonous, he can firmly lock a victim in his massive jaws.

The Boitatá particularly enjoys feasting on eyeballs. It is said that the more eyeballs the creature eats, the brighter his own eyes blaze!

AT A GLANCE

WHERE IN THE WORLD? Brazil

APPEARANCE: Fiery body, burning eyes

LAIR: Thick forest

BEHAVIOR: Ferocious and hungry

DRAGON POWER: Eyes light up the dark

VRITRA

 The evil Vritra had ninety-nine enormous coils. His body was so vast that it stretched right across the mountains of India. This huge monster could even block out the sun and turn day into night.

 Vritra's jaws were enormous. He once swallowed the Indian god Indra whole in one mighty gulp. The other gods were furious and forced Vritra to vomit the god back out.

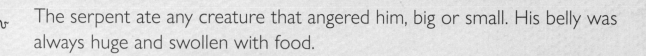 The serpent ate any creature that angered him, big or small. His belly was always huge and swollen with food.

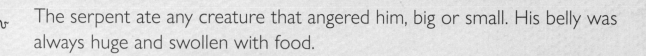 The creature's horrible hissing could be heard right across the land. His wicked laughter echoed across the sky and sounded like thunder.

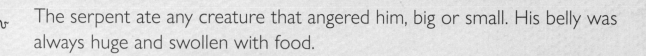 Vritra's name means "the enveloper," His rubbery body was incredibly flexible and stretchy. He could wrap himself around anything he chose and squeeze it tightly in his ninety-nine coils.

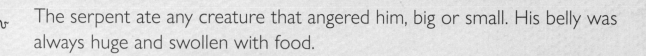 Vritra once drank all the world's water, causing terrible suffering. He held back rivers and sucked all the moisture from the skies. The god Indra killed Vritra with a mighty thunderbolt, and all the waters came gushing back out.

AT A GLANCE

WHERE IN THE WORLD? India

APPEARANCE: Huge body and jaws

LAIR: Mountaintops

BEHAVIOR: Wicked and loathsome

DRAGON POWER: Ninety-nine superstrong coils

PHAYA NAGA

- Phaya nagas are among the most magnificent dragons in the world. The green and golden scales of these river serpents glint like jewels just beneath the water's surface.

- These dragons live in the Mekong River. This mighty river runs through several countries in Southeast Asia.

- A phaya naga silently winds its body through the river like an eel. It can move both forward and backward.

- The people who live around the Mekong River see the phaya naga as a protector. They both respect and fear the dragon's great power.

- The stunning crest on this dragon's head is its crowning glory. The male's crest is much larger than the female's, and helps the creature to attract a mate.

AT A GLANCE

WHERE IN THE WORLD? Southeast Asia

APPEARANCE: Shimmering, crested

LAIR: Waters of the Mekong River

BEHAVIOR: Protects the river

DRAGON POWER: Breathes out fireballs

The female lays her eggs at the river's edge. They are so beautiful that they could easily be mistaken for precious stones. Beware of taking one home, though, or you might find you have a baby dragon on your hands.

Each year, around the night of the first full moon in October, amazing fireballs rise up from the Mekong River in Thailand. Thousands gather to watch the sight, which is said to be the fiery breath of a phaya naga.

THE TARASQUE

This extraordinary dragon had the head and mane of a lion, six stocky legs, and a turtlelike shell. Fire shot from his blazing eyes, and his hot breath burned everything around him.

The dragon's deadliest weapon was his lashing tail. At its tip was a venomous stinger, like a scorpion's.

The Tarasque lived more than eight hundred years ago in a deep forest in the south of France. He attacked any creature that crossed his path. His hooked claws were so sharp, they could slice through metal.

Many people tried to kill the Tarasque, but it seemed impossible. He was a ferocious fighter, and the thick, spiked shell on his back was like a suit of armor.

The dragon was a good swimmer and could stay underwater for long periods of time. He sometimes hunted along the river Rhône, snatching people from the riverbank or making their boats sink.

The people of the region asked a saint called Martha to help them slay the Tarasque. She whispered soft words, and the dragon meekly followed her to a nearby village. The beast didn't fight back and was swiftly killed.

The French town of Tarascon is named after the Tarasque. Today, its people remember the creature twice a year by pulling a model of the dragon through the streets in a procession.

AT A GLANCE

WHERE IN THE WORLD? France

APPEARANCE: Lion's head, serpent's tail

LAIR: Dark forest

BEHAVIOR: Vicious and beastly

DRAGON POWER: Stinger on his tail

THE RAINBOW SERPENT

This fabulous serpent from Australia looks like an enormous python. His eyes flash like jewels under the hot sun, and his scales shimmer with all the colors of the rainbow.

The Aboriginal people of Australia tell a story about the Rainbow Serpent. They say that he created the mountains as he pushed his way out of the ground. Then he carved out the rivers and valleys as he dragged his body across the land.

The Rainbow Serpent lives in waterholes in the hot deserts of Australia. During the dry season, when the waterholes dry up, he burrows deep beneath the cracked mud.

The serpent brings rain and life to the land. But if angered, he can create terrible floods and violent storms or stop the rain altogether.

Two boys once took shelter in the serpent's mouth, mistaking it for a cave. The creature swallowed them but felt really guilty afterward. To show his sorrow, he hid in the sky as a beautiful rainbow.

Scientists discovered rock paintings showing the Rainbow Serpent in Arnhem Land in Australia. They are believed to be at least six thousand years old.

AT A GLANCE

WHERE IN THE WORLD? Australia

APPEARANCE: Rainbow-colored

LAIR: Beneath waterholes

BEHAVIOR: Controls the weather

DRAGON POWER: Can take the form of a rainbow

THE PIASA BIRD

The most horrifying thing about this enormous bird-dragon was his humanlike face. His menacing eyes blazed with hunger, and sharp fangs lined his gaping mouth.

The Piasa Bird lived on cliffs high above the great Mississippi River in what is now Illinois. The Illini Indians, who first lived there, gave the monster his name. It means "the bird that devours men".

This monster had antlers like a deer's, a green, scaly body, and a long fish's tail that wound right around his body. His powerful eyes could spot the tiniest movement from a great distance.

- The creature had a beard, like that of a tiger, beneath his chin.

- The monster prowled the skies by day and by night. He swooped down to grasp his human prey with his enormous, curved talons. Then he carried the meal back to his lair and greedily devoured it.

- The beating of the Piasa Bird's great wings was a sound that terrified people. It warned them that the monster was nearby, and they immediately ran for cover.

- The Illini people tricked the Piasa Bird. Twenty warriors hid in some bushes while their chief stood out in the open. The monster swooped down to attack the chief but was speared to death by the warriors.

AT A GLANCE

WHERE IN THE WORLD? North America

APPEARANCE: Human-faced, winged

LAIR: Cave in high cliffs

BEHAVIOR: Hungry and ferocious

DRAGON POWER: Could see for miles

THE AMARU

- An amaru has two very different heads. One is the graceful head of a llama, and the other is the snarling head of a puma.

- Amarus live in the Andes Mountains in South America. In Quechua, the ancient language of the Inca civilization, Amaru means "snake".

- These extraordinary dragons have long, snakelike bodies and the majestic wings of a bird of prey. Their colorful feathers make a dazzling sight as they soar high above the mountains.

- Lurking underground, these creatures live in hidden caves and deep lakes. They are attracted to water and come out of their lairs when there are heavy rains.

- After a rainstorm, an amaru can create beautiful rainbows. It rises up through the sunshine and forms a giant arch between two water springs. As it sucks up the water, a rainbow appears in the sky.

- If angered, an amaru flies up into the sky to create icy hailstorms. It blasts out powerful gusts of air that stir up shrieking gales and lightning storms.

- An amaru once battled against Pariacaca, the god of water. Pariacaca stabbed the amaru in the back with a golden staff, and the dragon was instantly turned to stone. The stony shape of the dragon is still there today.

AT A GLANCE

WHERE IN THE WORLD? South America

APPEARANCE: Two-headed, winged

LAIR: Caves and deep lakes

BEHAVIOR: Proud and majestic

DRAGON POWER: Creates rainbows and whips up storms

THE AMPHISBAENA

This strange-looking dragon has a head at each end of her body. While one head sleeps, the other is on guard.

The Amphisbaena sprang from the blood of a monster called Medusa. The Greek hero Perseus chopped off Medusa's head. The Amphisbaena rose from the blood that dripped from the head.

The dragon's four mesmerizing eyes flicker and shine like dancing flames. She can trick her enemies by slithering either forward or backward.

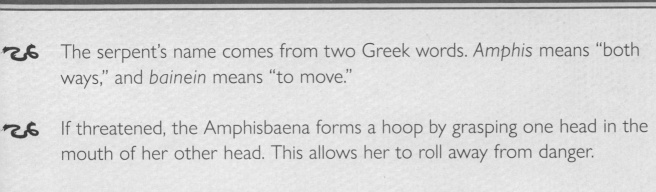 The serpent's name comes from two Greek words. *Amphis* means "both ways," and *bainein* means "to move."

If threatened, the Amphisbaena forms a hoop by grasping one head in the mouth of her other head. This allows her to roll away from danger.

The Amphisbaena is found in desert regions. She is sometimes called the Mother of Ants because she feasts on these insects. If given the opportunity, she will also eat the corpses of dead people.

This creature is believed to have healing powers. Her scales can be used to ward off colds and coughs. It is said that if a pregnant woman drapes the Amphisbaena around her neck, her baby will be born safe and well.

AT A GLANCE

WHERE IN THE WORLD? Libya, Africa

APPEARANCE: Twin-headed

LAIR: Desert hole

BEHAVIOR: Quick-witted and practical

DRAGON POWER: Magical healing powers

THE ETHIOPIAN DRAGON

- These magnificent dragons make their home in the rugged mountains of Ethiopia, in Africa. They are skilled and ferocious hunters and swoop down to attack elephants, wolves, and other large animals.

- The creatures have two powerful legs. Their gleaming, hooked talons are tougher than diamonds. They can tear and rip through prey and are strong enough to carry off a large elephant!

- Ethiopian dragons choose high cliff ledges for their lairs. Here, they build giant nests of branches and twigs, lined with soft rushes and grass.

- An Ethopian dragon's majestic wings allow it to soar high above the plains below. Like an eagle, it only beats its wings for short periods of time as it drifts and glides through the air.

AT A GLANCE

WHERE IN THE WORLD? Ethiopia, Africa

APPEARANCE: Two legs, tough talons

LAIR: Cliff-top ledge

BEHAVIOR: Crafty and intelligent

DRAGON POWER: Can lift an elephant

A female Ethiopian dragon lays several beautiful eggs in her nest. Just before hatching, the babies make a high-pitched singing sound. They use a tiny tooth at the end of their snouts to crack open their shells.

 Ethiopian dragons are extremely wise and intelligent creatures. Like a pack of wolves, they sometimes work together to hunt for prey.

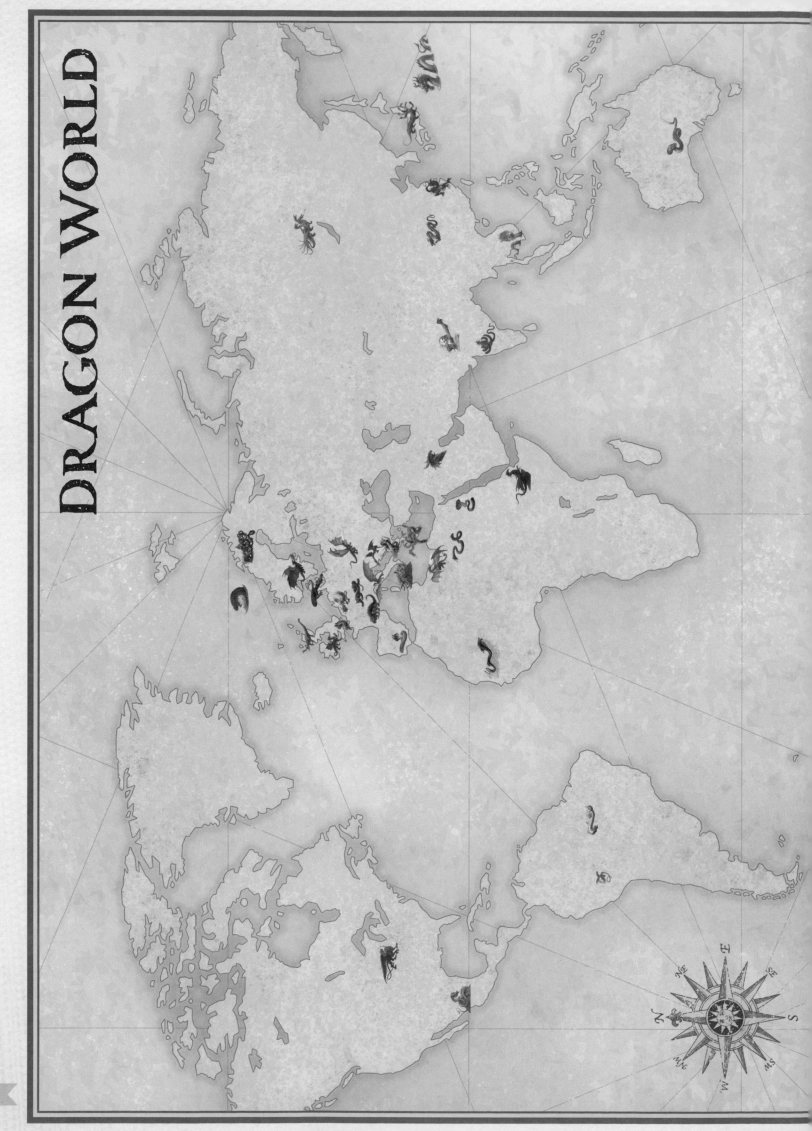